APR - - 2017

THE
GREAT
GOATINI

BALLET CAT

What's Your Favorite Favorite?

For Carol

Printed in Malaysia

Reinforced binding

First Edition, February 2017

10 9 8 7 6 5 4 3 2 1

FAC-029191-16316

Names: Shea, Bob.
Title: Ballet Cat : what's your favorite favorite? / Bob Shea.
Other titles: What's your favorite favorite?
Description: First hardcover edition. | Los Angeles ; New York :
Disney-Hyperion, 2017. | Includes bibliographical references and index. |
Summary: Ballet Cat and her cousin, Goat, try to outdo one another while
putting on a show for their grandmother.
Identifiers: LCCN 2015049797 | ISBN 9781484778098 (alk. paper)
Subjects: | CYAC: Grandmothers—Fiction. | Ballet dancing—Fiction. | Magic
Tricks—Fiction. | Cats—Fiction. | Goats—Fiction.
Classification: LCC PZ7.S53743 Wh 2017 | DDC [E]—dc23
LC record available at http://lccn.loc.gov/2015049797
www.DisneyBooks.com

BALLET CAT

What's Your Favorite Favorite?

Bob Shea

Leap Jump Twirl Leap Twirl Spin Jump Leap Leap Spin Leap Jump Leap Twirl Twirl

DISNEP · HYPERION

Los Angeles New York

Or I could
leap,

then twirl,

and jump.

Ballet and magic are both her favorite.
BALLET SHOW TODAY
THE GREAT GOATINI

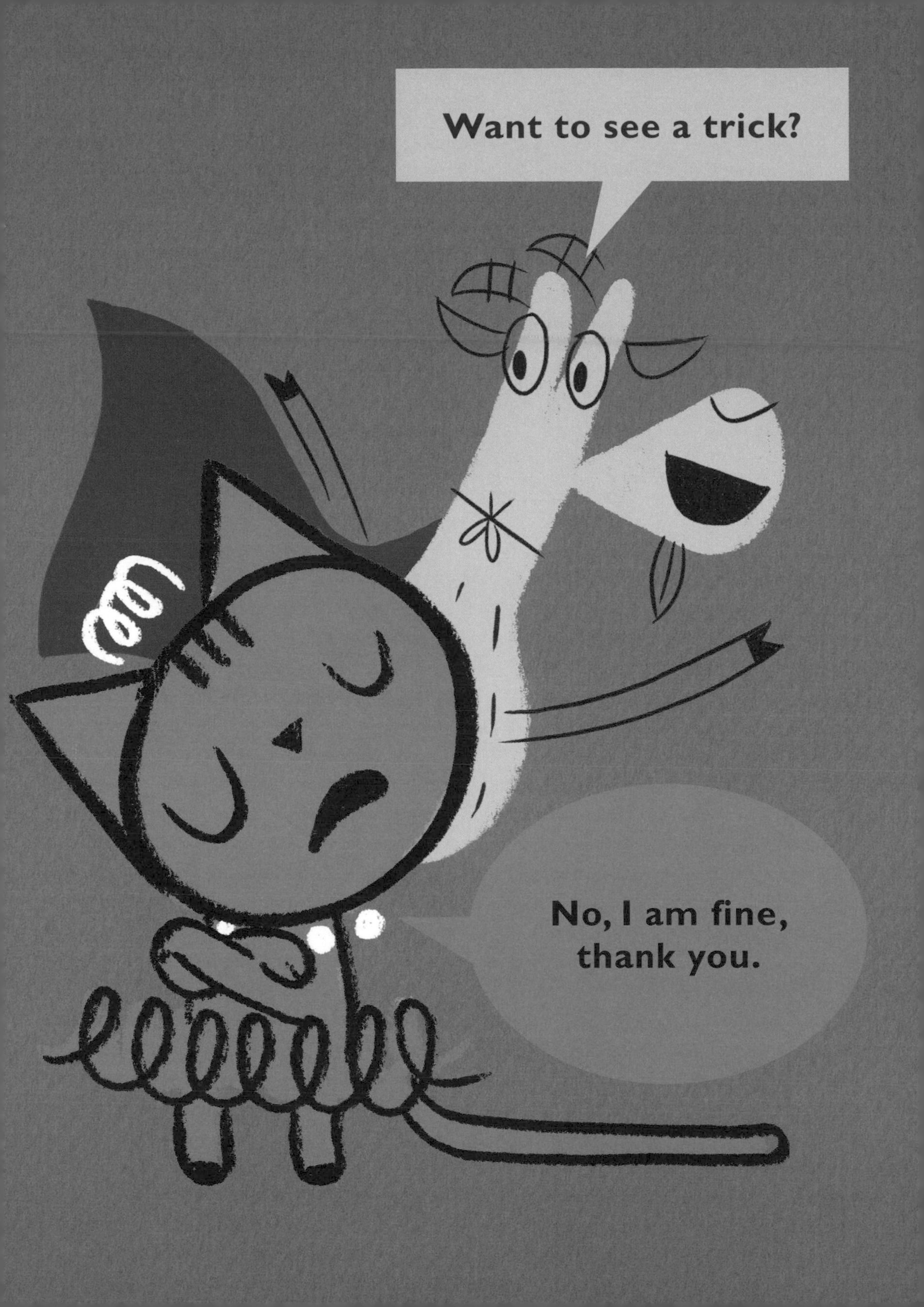
Want to see a trick?
No, I am fine, thank you.

dip,

jump!

Is it a baby picture of me in an "I love Grandma" shirt?

WOW!

How did you know?

Hello! Anyone home?

Grandma! It is time for our show!

Look, tea! And those dry cookies old people like.

Look, Grandma! A quarter! It was behind your ear!
Look, Grandma! A big leap!
25

Grandma! Grandma!
Grandma! Grandma!
Grandma!
Grandma!
Grandma!
Grandma!

Grandma?

Oh no.

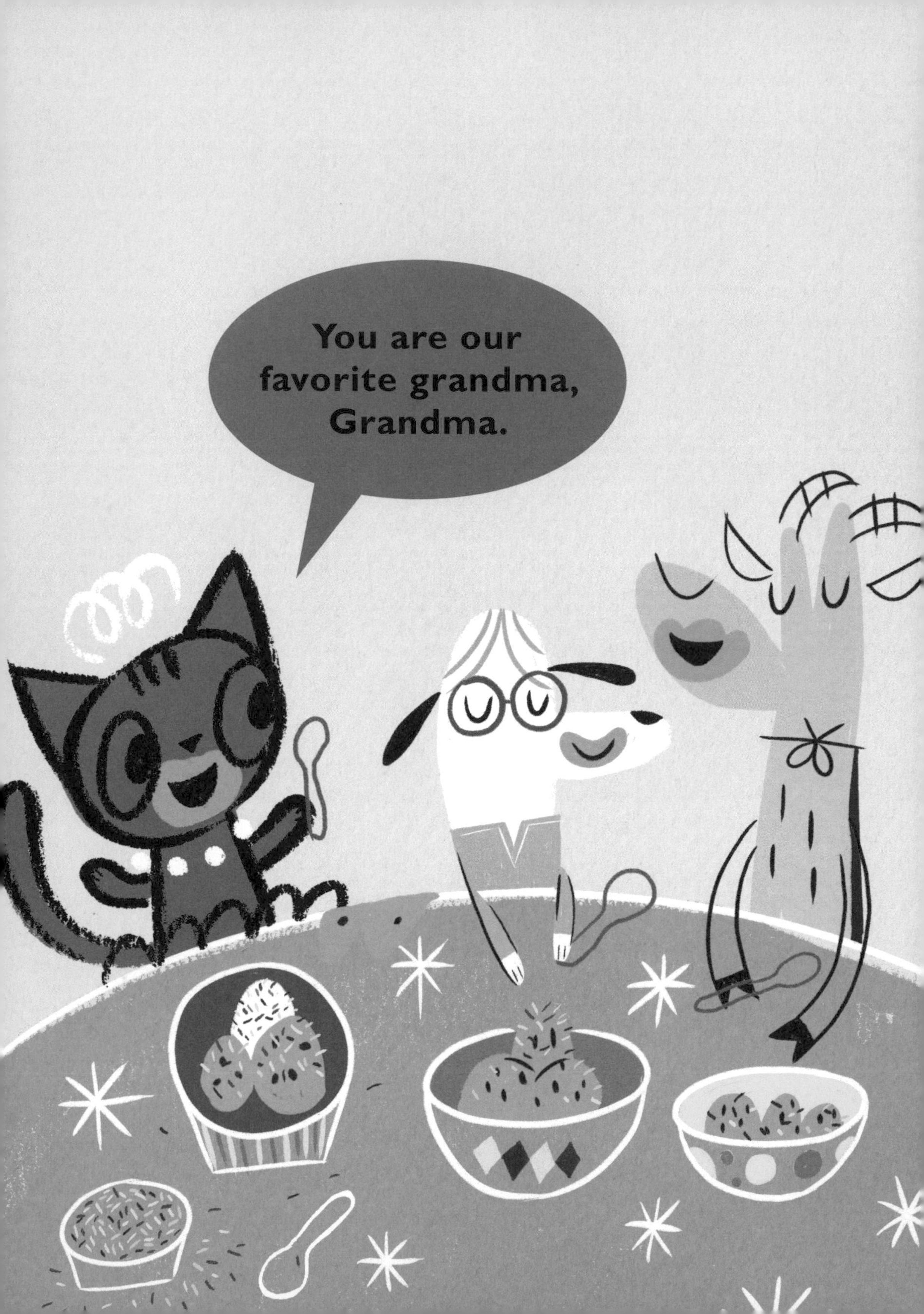
You are our favorite grandma, Grandma.